Emma Wyatt is a stay-at-home mum to her two boys, Harry and George. Her debut book has been inspired by Harry's incredible kindness and the heroic effort of the NHS during 2020/2021. When she is not writing short stories for her children, she has her wellies on exploring the Kent countryside where she lives.

Super Harry

EMMA WYATT

AUSTIN MACAULEY PUBLISHERS™
LONDON • CAMBRIDGE • NEW YORK • SHARJAH

Copyright © Emma Wyatt (2021)

A CIP catalogue record for this title is available from the British Library.

ISBN 9781398419551 (Paperback)
ISBN 9781398419568 (ePub e-book)

www.austinmacauley.com

First Published (2021)
Austin Macauley Publishers Ltd
25 Canada Square
Canary Wharf
London
E14 5LQ

For Harry and George

Harry rode his balance bike down his favourite track,

He waved to the tractor and the farmer waved right back.

Horses, donkeys, pigs and cows, he spotted as he rode,

"Look at me Mummy!" shouted Harry, as he went

into high—speed mode.

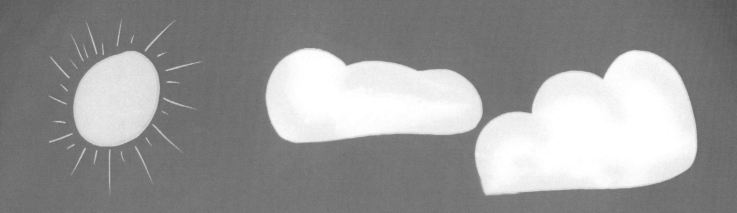

Harry pretends to be a SUPERHERO, flying through the air,

ZOOM, he's off to save the people as he whizzes here and there.

Everywhere seemed very quiet and Harry didn't know why,

Where are all the people? he wondered with a sigh.

Mummy saw that Harry was sad, as they stopped to have a snack,

"You see," Mummy explained, "the world is under attack.

There are lots of germs flying around making people sick,

Everyone must stay at home, as that will do the trick!

We need to give the scientists time to find a cure,

The world will then be mended and back to being pure."

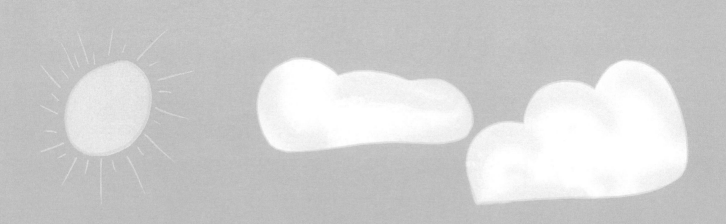

"We are in safe hands though, Harry, because the doctors are superheroes, like you.
Putting on their capes and saving people too.
The nurses wear their capes as well, showing everyone they care,
The carers too are superheroes as they have so much kindness to share."

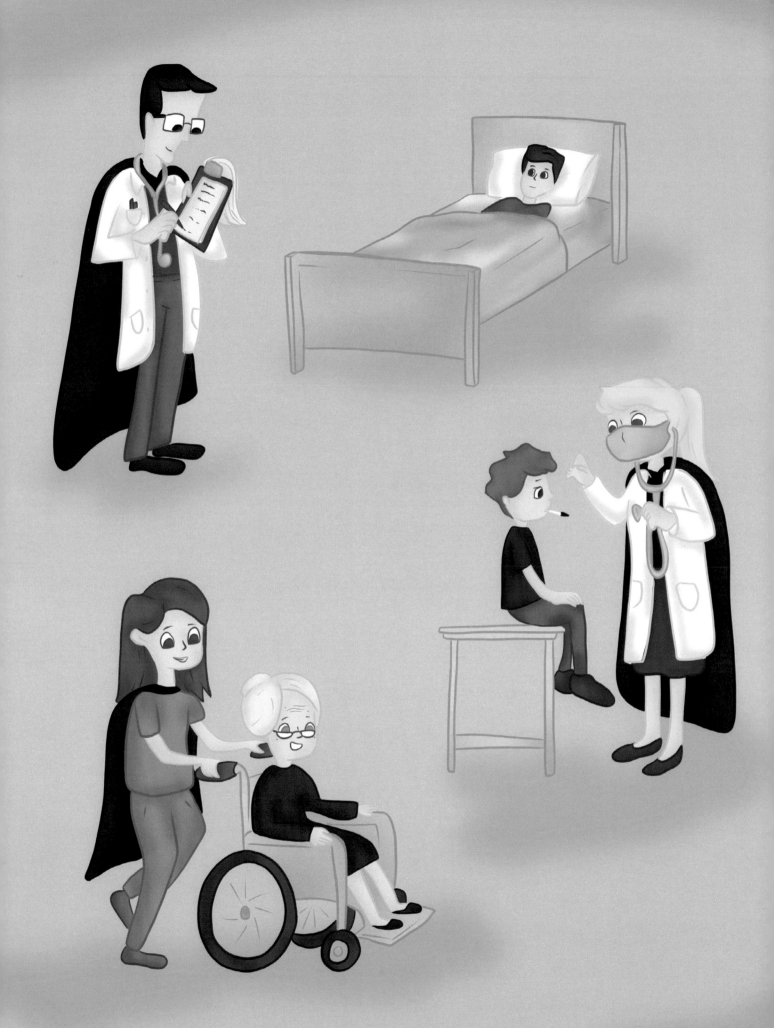

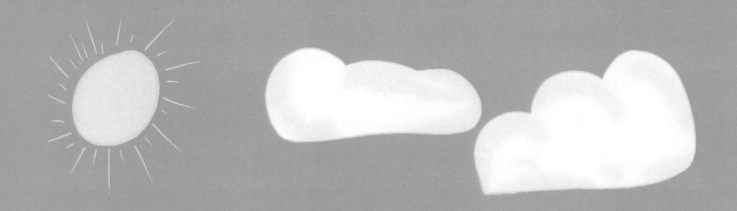

Harry pretends to be a SUPERHERO, flying through the air,

ZOOM, he's off to save the people as he whizzes here and there.

That night Harry decided to play with his doctors set,

Taking temperatures, listening to hearts but

he couldn't help feel upset.

"I want to help the doctors, the nurses and carers, it's true!

I know, I have an idea, I can be a superhero too!"

I 'll dress up as Super Harry and show everyone I know,

How I can ride my balance bike come wind or rain or snow!

I 'll get my friends and family, to sponsor me to ride,

And I 'll ride and ride and ride some more,

I 'll be Super Harry with pride!

"Well done Super Harry, you 're a star!"

his friends cheer aloud,

"Keep riding Super Harry, you can do it!

You are making us so proud!"

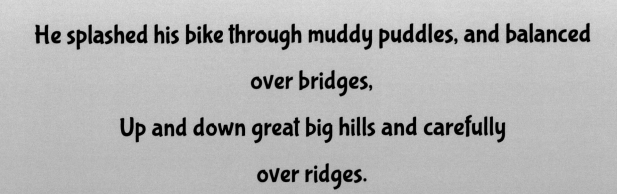

He splashed his bike through muddy puddles, and balanced
over bridges,
Up and down great big hills and carefully
over ridges.

SUPER HARRY is a SUPERHERO, flying through the air,

ZOOM, he's off to save the people as he whizzes here and there.

22

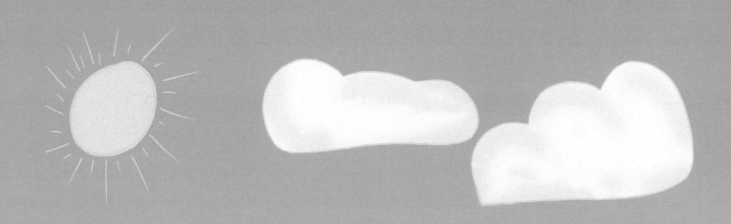

After many days of riding, Super Harry's adventure comes to
an end,

He is very proud of the money he raised, so he thanks his family
and friends.

The money Harry raised has helped all the doctors, nurses
and carers,

The porters, cleaners, chefs and all the superhero cape wearers.

One day the germs disappear, the scientists save the day,

The world went back to normal; all the children came out to play.

"One day I want to be a doctor, porter, nurse or carer,

I want to save the people and be a real superhero cape wearer."

Harry pretends to be a SUPERHERO, flying through the air

ZOOM, he's off to save the people as he whizzes here and there.